Sacrifice

of the

Dragon

Marked by the Dragon Book 5

RICHARD FIERCE

Dragonfire Press

Cover design by germancreative.

Cover art by Nimesh Niyomal

ISBN: 978-1-958354-41-4

CONTENTS

MAP

1

The air was hot and dry, and Mina shielded the sun from her eyes as Gedrith flew above The Long Sands. A sand wyrm had been spotted on the fringes of the Enclave's domain, and as part of her continued training, the two of them had been tasked with scouting the area.

Mina watched the sand dunes, looking for the telltale signs that signaled the underground movement of the beast. She'd learned much in the two weeks since the fall of Velbridge, and yet she couldn't shake the feeling that she was still too ill-equipped to be a dragon rider.

"It there!" Areg shouted, pointing. He stood in the saddle behind her, his arm outstretched past her head.

She followed his fingers to the ground and saw it clearly. A bulge in the dunes that rose and fell, swaying side to side, like an enormous desert serpent. Mina swallowed hard and clenched her jaw.

Do you see it? She asked Gedrith.

Yes.

What do you think it's doing here?

I do not know, but it doesn't matter. We must kill it.

Mina was afraid he was going to say that. Her only encounter with sand wyrms had been terrifying, and they'd had the aid of many dragons then.

Should we alert the others?

There isn't time. If we leave, it may get away.

Is that a bad thing?

The only good sand wyrm is a dead one, Gedrith rumbled.

The smell of orchids filled her nostrils, and she knew he was disappointed with her fear and reluctance. She ignored the urge to apologize.

We need to draw it to the surface, she said.

Without offering a reply, Gedrith dove down sharply. Areg latched onto her shoulders, gripping her tightly with his small hands. Despite his diminutive size, he was much stronger than he looked. The air whipped past them, pulling at her hair and rippling her shirt wildly. The dry air stung her eyes, and she leaned forward and squinted.

When the ground was only a few feet away, Gedrith pulled up and leveled out, using his massive wings to catch the air and slow his descent. He glided over the shifting sand and raked his rear claws down deep. Catching on the flesh of the wyrm, Gedrith's bulk shuddered briefly, but it was enough force that Areg crashed into Mina and the two of them fell from Gedrith's back.

Mina gasped in surprise and pain as she tumbled

along the dune. Once her body stopped rolling, she sat up and spat grit from her mouth. A glance at herself didn't reveal any injuries, but she'd probably be sore tomorrow. Staggering to her feet, she looked around for Areg. The elf was a dozen paces away, already on his feet with his sword drawn.

Are you hurt? Gedrith asked.

He flew over her, his shadow temporarily blotting out the sun.

I don't think so. Where's the wyrm?

Get to the top of the hill.

His lack of an answer told her they were in danger. She ran up the dune, pumping her legs furiously, but the sand pulled at her boots, slowing her down. Areg raced past her, his small feet skimming the sand so lightly he barely left any footsteps. If all elves were as agile, it was a wonder they weren't the only ones allowed to bond with dragons. Then again, he was the only elf she'd ever seen, which was curious.

By the time she reached the top of the hill, sweat slicked her skin and she had trouble pulling her sword from the sheath at her side. The ground trembled beneath her, and the sand vibrated, causing miniature landslides to pour down the dune. A moment later, Areg tackled her, knocking her on the flat of her back.

Before she could question him, the ground where she'd been standing erupted. The head of the sand wyrm, its maw opened wide, burst forth, showering her and the elf with sand and spittle. Areg had saved her life. She scrambled onto her feet and drew her sword.

"Thank you," she huffed.

Areg nodded, turning to watch the path of the wyrm. Mina did the same. The beast continued down the other side of the dune, disappearing back below the ground, though the bulge it left behind was a clear sign of where it was going. It made a wide turn and circled back.

"What do we do?" she asked, panic threatening to overwhelm her common sense.

"Kill," Areg replied simply, smiling.

"How?"

The elf shook his blade.

"Yes, with a sword, obviously. I mean, *how* do we kill it with a sword? What exactly do I need to stab?"

"Heart," he said.

Mina remembered Gedrith's words from their battle with the wyrm king.

"It's encased in bone and muscle, so how do I penetrate it?"

"No, wyrm king only. This easy."

At Mina's baleful look, Areg shrugged. "More easy," he clarified.

When the elf had killed the wyrm king, he'd been swallowed by the creature. The only way to kill them was from the inside. Mina shuddered at the thought.

"I'll draw its attention, and you get in there and kill it," she said.

Areg shook his head. "You."

"Me? No, I can't do it."

"Can. Hold breath. Stab heart. Easy."

Mina watched the swell in the sand as it drew nearer, and realization dawned on her. This was part of her training, another test of her abilities and what she'd learned. Why hadn't Gedrith warned her?

"If it's so easy, why did you push me out of the way?"

"Not prepared. Wrong place." Areg motioned with his hands, indicating she would have been dismembered by the creature. The trembling of the ground ran up the length of Mina's legs, drawing her focus back to the approaching wyrm. It was time to stop questioning herself. She was no longer a slave, but a dragon rider.

The first dragon rider in a thousand years. The only *true* dragon rider.

Mina gripped the hilt of her sword tightly and pushed the fear aside. The bulge in the sand came straight toward her. She centered herself with it and had to scream at herself not to flee. The wyrm broke the surface of the ground, and time seemed to still. The creature's mouth opened, revealing a torrent of saliva that dripped onto the sand.

Time returned to normal, and Mina brought her sword up in front of her, lunging forward into the wyrm's mouth. It swallowed her, plunging her into wet darkness. She ran ahead blindly, holding her breath as Areg had instructed. The fleshy walls inside of the wyrm pulsed and constricted around her. Her lungs burned intensely, and she feared she was going to suffocate.

Where is the heart? she cried out.

You will know it when you see it, Gedrith replied. *Keep going.*

Mina forced herself to put one foot in front of the other, hacking at the wyrm's insides as she did so. If the creature felt any pain from it, she couldn't tell. Her chest tightened and the burning in her lungs was almost too much to bear. Why did she have to hold her breath, anyway?

She gasped and heaved in a deep lungful of air. The foul smell of decay assailed her and she understood why Areg told her not to breathe. It made her eyes water, but she felt something thrumming ahead. It was powerful, and she assumed it was the heart. A few more steps forward, and a reddish-pink light became visible. The light pulsed in conjunction with the vibrations, giving her no doubt that it was indeed the wyrm's heart.

Mina pointed the tip of the sword at the light and spread her feet, bracing herself. She thrusted the blade with all her might. It cut through the layers of flesh easily, and the sword sank in up to the hilt. The wyrm shuddered around her, and she was aware that the creature came to an abrupt halt.

The deed was done, and now she needed to escape. She remembered Areg had cut his way out of the wyrm king's side, and so she began hacking at the fleshy wall to her left. Warm, wet liquid coated her arms, and she assumed it was blood. Ignoring her revulsion, she swung the sword over and over until daylight was visible and she burst out onto the sand. From her periphery, she saw Areg running down to the dune toward her.

"Did it!" he shouted triumphantly. "Did it!"

A shadow passed overhead and a moment later, Gedrith landed nearby, his powerful wings stirring up the desert sand. Mina dropped her sword and fell to her knees, covered in blood and other things she'd rather not consider.

Very good, Gedrith said. *You have passed the Enclave's final test.*

Mina remained silent for a moment, her thoughts a scrambled mess. She looked from the dragon to Areg, then wiped some entrails from her cheek.

"I need a bath," she huffed.

2

Sunlight filtered into the cell from the narrow window near the ceiling. It was the only thing that marked the passage of time. Caden used the edge of his right shackle to scrape a line on the wall. It joined the other thirteen, and he stared at the lines in silence. It had been a fortnight since Mina had left him here to rot, but it felt much longer than that.

With the absence of Lireth in his mind, it was as though a fog had lifted. His thoughts felt like his own, and it was an odd feeling. It was almost as if he was experiencing things for the first time, yet he knew that was not true. Had Lireth taken control of his thoughts, or did he simply feel this way because of the distance that separated them?

It was impossible to tell.

The former would explain why Mina had turned against him, but it was her dragon that was evil. Wasn't he? It all made his head throb, and he pushed the thoughts aside. A guard must have brought breakfast at some point, for a wooden bowl filled with soup sat on the floor near the cell door. Caden crawled along the floor and grabbed it, lifting the bowl to his nose and sniffing its contents.

It was a sweet, earthy aroma, and he could smell hints of celery and carrots. The food was better than nothing, but he longed for eggs, fresh bread, and meat. He downed the soup and grimaced. It was cold, and the flavor was lacking. Whoever was cooking the food didn't know what they were doing.

Something *clinked* against the bars of the window, and Caden looked up. Nothing was there. He had lost Lireth already. Was he now losing his mind? A dark shape flew past the window, and a moment later, a dull thud echoed into the cell. Caden rose to his feet and stilled his breath. He could hear muffled voices on the other side of the wall, but he couldn't discern their words.

He took a couple of steps closer to the wall and froze, tilting his head to the side and listening intently.

"Give it to me, you fool. It isn't that hard."

Caden looked at the window again just in time to see a thin, cylindrical-shaped item come through the bars. Before he could think to move out of the way, it struck him across his right eye. He fell on his back with a gasp of pain and pressed his hand to his face. There was no blood, but it stung like fire.

He sat up and glanced around. The cylinder had rolled up against the wall. He grabbed it and held it up, wincing as a flash of pain erupted near his cheekbone. The pain lessened to a dull ache, and he ran his fingers over the smooth wood. At the top was a cap. He pulled it off and looked inside to see a rolled parchment. Sliding his finger in, he fished it out and unfurled it. There were only five words written on it:

Stand back from the wall.

Caden set the letter and container aside and massaged his face as he scooted back from the wall. Who was out there? And what did they want? A grinding noise filled the cell, and the sharp edge of a metal tool ripped through the stone wall. It cut a rough square shape, and someone on the other side pushed the stones into the cell. Daylight flooded through the opening, blinding Caden. He held his hand up to block the light and saw the outline of a figure climb through the hole in the wall.

"My lord," the figure extended a hand. "We've come to rescue you."

Caden accepted the help and looked into the reptilian face of Bast. A confusing swirl of emotions washed over him. The last time Caden had seen the draman, he tried to kill him, thinking he was a traitor. An unexplainable guilt filled his gut.

"Bast," he finally said. "I'm sorry."

"We must go before they realize you are gone."

Bast grabbed the shackle on his right hand and snapped it off, then did the same with the other. Caden rubbed his sore wrists, still confused.

"Why are you here?"

"I told you already."

"No, I know *why* you are here, but why are *you* here? I'm sure you despise me."

"I do not," Bast replied. "There was much on your shoulders. We can talk about these things later. Come."

The draman climbed back through the hole, and Caden glanced around the cell. He'd finally resigned himself to dying alone here in the dungeon, but now freedom was right in front of him. Did he deserve to be free? Lireth had saved his life and bound herself to him, yet he had failed her when she needed him most.

"My lord, please. Our mistress needs our help. She is being held captive by the Enclave."

"Our mistress," Caden repeated.

Perhaps she would show him mercy when he arrived with the draman to break her out. It was the only thing he could hope for, and it was certainly better than rotting in Lord Culver's dungeon. Caden slipped through the damaged wall and out into the fresh air. The warmth of the sun on his skin was a welcome change from the cold stones of his cell.

"Thank you," Caden said, looking from Bast to the dozen other draman who had aided in his rescue. "I failed you all, but I will do my best to restore your trust in me."

Bast waved his clawed hand. "We are all guilty of failure."

"Is this everyone?"

"No, the others are gathered in the woods where we were camped before the attack on Velbridge."

"How many?"

"Twelve hundred strong."

Relief washed over Caden. He was thankful

they hadn't all died in the battle. "What of Lireth's allies? The other dragons?"

"Gone, I'm afraid. They fled when Lord D'Lance used his magic to stop her."

"And Mina, the girl, her dragon slew Lord D'Lance?"

Bast chuckled. "No. The girl did."

That gave Caden pause. Mina had killed Lord D'Lance? That meant she had … saved him. And Lireth. That was intriguing. And … unexpected.

"I see."

"We should get moving," Bast said. "We can discuss these things while we walk."

3

After Mina had thoroughly washed the grime and sand wyrm filth from herself, she walked along the corridors, the pattering of her bare feet echoing softly off the glass walls. Word had spread quickly among the dragons that she had single-handedly killed a sand wyrm. She still found it hard to believe she had succeeded.

Lost in her thoughts, she found herself standing outside the chamber that served as Lireth's prison cell. She stared through the glass, watching the dragon stalk back and forth across the cave. She was enormous, and the dragon seemed all the larger in the confined space. Her claws scraped the floor in her pacing, and the scent of saffron drifted in the air, reaching Mina's nostrils even through the cave wall. Lireth's fury had yet to abate. Although the wall was thin, it had proved to be impenetrable. The myriad of scratch marks on the other side was proof of that.

When Lireth's pacing brought her near, Mina turned away. She had watched the creature long enough. Firm steps echoed off the walls, and she saw Areg approaching.

"What doin'?"

"Nothing," she replied.

The diminutive elf still wore his leather armor and carried his sword at his waist. When she'd first met him, he'd startled her as she had never seen an elf before. His short stature and pale complexion differed from any human she'd ever met. His odd speech, the result of a horrific accident, added to his peculiar appearance. Despite all that, Mina found him to be cute in a platonic way, though she would never tell him that. He was a fierce warrior, his endearing appearance deceiving.

"Ready?"

"I need to get my boots," she replied, lifting her right foot and wiggling her toes.

"We go."

Mina nodded and walked with the elf to her chambers. She slipped her boots on and belted her sword around her waist.

"Do you think the draman will come for Lireth? I know she is too far away to speak with them, but they are still connected to her."

Areg shrugged his small shoulders. "Foolish. Dragons stronger."

"True," she said.

It had been two weeks since Lireth's imprisonment, two weeks since Caden had been locked away in Lord Culver's dungeon. Mina had thought about him every day since she'd left him there. They had been friends, and at one time, she even hoped it would blossom into more than friendship, but Lireth's bond with him had corrupted his mind and turned him against her.

She spent her days training with Areg and strengthening her bond with Gedrith. Again, she considered the inadequacy she felt, though slaying the sand wyrm had alleviated the feeling somewhat. She was the first dragon rider in a thousand years, but it was all a coincidental accident. She wasn't born a warrior, nor was she a leader. Until recently, she'd been a slave to Lord Klodian, leading him on dragon hunts so he could kill the creatures for sport.

Now, she was living among them as if her past wasn't full of blood and death. Gedrith had forgiven her, but the sins of her past still haunted her. She knew she needed to forgive herself, but she didn't know how.

She and Areg walked up the slope that led out of the underground caves and into the sunlight. The air was hotter and drier than earlier, if that were possible, and the smell of dust was overwhelming. The scenery wasn't much different from Klodian Keep, aside from the lack of human buildings. She wondered how Lord Klodian was doing, then pushed the thought from her mind. It didn't matter. *He* didn't matter.

Gedrith sunbathed while waiting for them, his massive wings outstretched. He lifted his head as they approached.

The Enclave is impressed with your victory over the sand wyrm.

Did they send you out here to tell me that?

No. I wanted to see your progress with the blade.

Mina unsheathed her sword and took a few practice swings.

I have learned many things, but I still don't think I am fit for battle.

You are too hard on yourself, Gedrith said.

I must be.

Why?

Mina inhaled a deep breath. *To atone for my sins.*

Is your name Avera now, that you have such power?

That gave her pause. *I do not fancy myself a goddess, if that's what you mean.*

Then let go of your past, for only the gods can erase history.

Mina stabbed the tip of her blade into the ground and knelt, grabbing a handful of sand. She let it sift through her fingers as she contemplated his words. Perhaps he was right. Her mistakes plagued her thoughts, but if she was the only one thinking about them, then it amounted to nothing more than self-torture. She stood and grabbed her sword, turning to face Areg.

What am I training for? she asked Gedrith. *Lord D'Lance is dead.*

Do you believe that he was the only force of evil in the world?

No.

Good, I would be worried otherwise. As a dragon rider, it is your duty to protect those who cannot defend themselves.

How is one person supposed to protect everyone else?

With help, of course. Mine, as well as the Enclave's.

Will there be more like me? More dragon riders?

Gedrith remained silent for a moment. *The Enclave has not decided on that yet. It will depend on you.*

Me? I thought I proved myself to them already.

You did, but it is not as simple as that.

What do you mean?

Focus on your training, Gedrith said.

Mina stared at him. There was something he wasn't telling her.

We are bound as one, are we not? If you expect me to trust you, then you must trust me as well.

Very well. I did not want to worry you, but I will not hide anything from you. The Enclave has been keeping an eye on things in the Dominions. Lireth's draman are slowly regrouping.

Regrouping? Are they plotting to come for her?

That remains to be seen, but it would not be wise for them to come here.

Yes, but we have already seen what madness Lireth can accomplish inside people's minds. Danger will not keep them from doing what is foolish. They need to be stopped before they do anything rash. What is the Enclave going to do about them?

As it stands, nothing, Gedrith replied. *They are not a threat to us.*

Mina wasn't so sure of that, but she didn't argue with him.

Unless something changes, you will stay here and continue learning.

And if something changes? Then what?

Then you and I will deal with it.

Mina nodded. *Very well.* She turned back to Areg. "Are you ready?"

Areg smiled. "Come on."

Mina lifted her blade and lunged forward.

4

A flood of emotions washed over Caden as he walked into the camp with Bast. Draman were working busily, some cooking and others moving supplies to large tents used for storage. He was glad to see so many of them had survived the battle in Velbridge. Bast led him to a pavilion that was modestly sized, though larger than most of the other tents.

"This one is yours," he said. Bast seemed to have genuinely forgiven him, but Caden couldn't help feeling guilty about his prior actions.

"I am sorry for questioning your loyalty," he said, looking at the draman. "My mind was clouded by many things."

"I do not hold any ill feelings toward you, my lord. Even if I did, our mistress has put you in charge of her forces, and I would never disobey her commands."

Caden nodded. He believed Bast, which made him again question why he thought the draman had been a traitor. An uncomfortable thought hovered at the back of his mind, but he dared not acknowledge it.

"What's left of Velbridge?" he asked.

"The fires destroyed much, and the people ransacked what remained before fleeing to safer places. We've already scoured the ruins for supplies, but there was little that was usable. What you see here is all we have."

"What of the other Dominions? Have any of the lords tried to claim the Dracan for themselves?"

"No. The High Prince sent soldiers to patrol the dominion and ensure order. We've kept hidden since they arrived."

Caden was unsurprised by the news, though he knew little about the High Prince. He suspected the man was collecting the details of what had happened, and once he discovered what Lord D'Lance had been plotting, he would probably be relieved the man was dead.

"What of the other dragons? Those who came to aid our mistress?"

Bast growled. "They fled north when the tides of battle shifted. Cowards."

"I don't disagree with that assessment, but we are going to need their help to find the Enclave. With our limited numbers, it will be impossible to find their home in The Long Sands."

"Do you want me to send some men to seek them out?"

"No," Caden replied. "I will do it."

"You've just returned to us, my lord. Is it wise for you to leave?"

Caden didn't like the idea of tracking down dragons on his own, but he felt by doing so would prove his devotion to Lireth. That, and perhaps she would be more merciful to him after she was free. He reached through the bond, but it faded into obscurity and there was nothing at the other end.

"I will return as soon as I can. In the meantime, focus on finding food and water. We'll need plenty of both if we're going to march through the desert."

"As you command," Bast said, bowing his head.

A realization dawned on Caden, and he frowned. "With Lord D'Lance dead, there will not be any new draman. We will need to find a way to strengthen our numbers."

"When the castle was destroyed, we found female draman that Lord D'Lance was keeping in the dungeon. It seems he did not limit his experiments only to the soldiers."

"What does this mean?" Caden asked.

"It is yet to be seen, but I believe we will be able to breed more of our kind in natural ways."

"I think Lireth will be happy to hear that."

"I would not want to give her false hope, my lord. As I said, it remains to be seen."

"You are right, my friend. Let us not mention it until we know for certain."

They stood in silence for a moment, and then Bast said, "It is good to have you back among us."

"It is good to be back. Thank you again for rescuing me, though I do not deserve your kindness after what I did."

"It is forgiven," Bast replied, waving a clawed hand. "Do not mention it again. It is in the past now. When will you leave?"

"Soon," Caden said. "I need something to eat, and then I will go. Lireth has been gone too long as it is, and I do not want her imprisoned any longer than is necessary."

"Until you return then, my lord." Bast bowed his head again and turned to leave.

"I told you before to call me Caden. Nothing has changed that."

"Very well. Until you return, Caden."

Bast left to attend to his duties, and Caden got some food from a group of draman who were cooking meat over a large fire. It was impossible to tell what sort of creature was on the spit, but when Caden put a piece of the meat into his mouth, he immediately recognized the taste of deer. He complimented the draman on the meal, then went to his tent.

Being back among them felt much like being home, though he supposed it truly was his home. They were all servants to Lireth, and in that shared bond, they were close. One could even say they were family, in a way. Caden's eyes roamed the camp as he considered his path forward. Searching out the other dragons was risky, especially if they flamed him before hearing him out.

For a brief moment, he almost lost his nerve, but he pushed his doubts aside. There was no sense in waiting. The quicker he returned, the quicker they could get to The Long Sands to free Lireth. It seemed an eternity since he had heard her voice or felt her presence. Something deep inside him stirred, and he wondered if she could feel him even if he couldn't feel her.

Caden turned away from his tent and went to the pavilion that served as an armory. He grabbed a chainmail shirt and pulled it over his head, then chose a sword that was sharp and well-balanced. They would do nothing against a dragon, but there was no telling what sort of trouble he might run into considering the dominion was still recovering. High Prince or not, people would resort to the darkest of deeds to ensure they could eat.

With that thought in mind, he also grabbed a short dagger and tucked it into his belt. Satisfied he was suitably armed, Caden strapped a leather satchel over his shoulder and returned to the draman who were cooking. They offered him enough rations to last a week, but he felt guilty accepting that much and refused, taking only a couple of days' worth instead.

Content he had everything he needed, he left the camp and trudged north.

5

Mina sat atop a hill, taking a break from sparring with Areg. She sipped water from a canteen and stared at the rolling dunes that stretched to the horizon. Gedrith joined her, and the two sat in silence until Mina voiced a question that had been on her mind since the battle in Velbridge.

How did I breathe fire?

Gedrith issued a deep rumble that shook the sand and sent a miniature avalanche down the hill.

When the bond is strong enough, riders and their dragons can share their senses and abilities. You needed help, and I gave you power over my flames.

Mina stood and opened her mouth. After a moment, she frowned and turned to look at Gedrith.

Nothing happened. Can I not breathe fire at will?

Yes, if I allow it.

What do you mean?

You have access to me and my power through the bond, but I must allow you to use it.

Let me use your fire, please. I want to see how it works.

Very well.

Mina turned away from the dragon and opened her mouth again. She focused on the bond and called on Gedrith's flames. Her throat grew warm, but only a small flicker of orange flew out of her mouth.

It will take time to master the ability, Gedrith said.

Then how did I do it so easily in Velbridge?

Desperation made the connection more powerful. It is difficult to recreate that urgency without genuine fear.

Some things took time. That was the way of the world, even with magic it seemed. Mina had plenty of time, as there was nothing to do but train. Unless a new enemy arose, anyway. She licked her lips and closed her mouth, then sat down in the sand and leaned back against Gedrith.

I feel out of place here, she admitted. *I'm surrounded by dragons.*

Areg is not a dragon.

I know, but he's not a human.

Do you miss being among other humans?

Yes.

Despite the way many of them are?

It sounds strange, I'm sure, but yes.

Even when Lucius was alive, I was always around other dragons. I cannot understand your desire because I have never experienced it myself, but I do not think it is wise for you to leave here.

Although she missed her own kind, Mina didn't want to leave. Not without Gedrith. He was as much a part of her as any of her limbs. She smiled as she thought back to the first time they had met. He was about to kill Lord Klodian, and she heard him speak. Much had changed since then, and some of it was for the better.

She shielded her eyes from the sun and looked down to where Areg was. The elf was still practicing his swordplay, whirling this way and that, his blade flashing under the sun with every slash. It was nice to have someone to learn from. It helped with the boredom, but it also took her mind off things, such as her loneliness.

Perhaps it would be beneficial for you to have human companionship here, Gedrith said.

The Enclave would allow that?

It will take some convincing, but I do not see why they would take issue with it, especially if it is someone open to bonding with a dragon.

Mina abruptly sat up and turned to look at Gedrith. *Another dragon rider? I thought you said the Enclave hadn't decided on that yet?*

They haven't. I do not speak for the Enclave, but they trust my wisdom. This could be an opportunity to show them it is time to rebuild the riders.

Is the world ready for that?

We shall see, Gedrith replied.

More dragon riders? Mina relished the idea of having others who could understand her struggles, but she also feared what would happen if the wrong person were to bond with a dragon. Gedrith sensed her unease.

The Enclave fears the same thing, but we must not let that keep us from the world. We are part of it despite how much we try to isolate ourselves.

The two were silent for a moment, and Mina wondered if the Enclave would agree to have another human here. She didn't think so, but it wouldn't hurt to ask. The question was, who would she want to come here? The obvious answer was Caden, but she pushed the thought from her mind. Having spent most of her life as a slave, she didn't have any friends. The only person she had ever slightly trusted was …

Thais wouldn't come here, would she? Mina hadn't thought about her since she'd left Klodian Keep. With Lord D'Lance dead, had her parents gained their freedom?

Do you have someone in mind?

Gedrith's question broke her reverie.

I may have someone. Her name is Thais. She's a soldier, but I don't know if she would want to come here.

Is there no one else?

No. She didn't hesitate with her answer. *She would make a good dragon rider. She's strong and smart.*

Gedrith hummed in thought. *Very well. I will speak to the Enclave. I cannot guarantee anything, but perhaps they will allow it.*

Mina stood and stretched, ready to continue sparring with Areg. She laid a hand on Gedrith's snout, feeling the rough texture of his scales against her skin.

Thank you. Will you keep the connection to your flames open for me? I want to practice breathing fire.

Yes, but take heed. Until you have learned to control the fire, you risk hurting yourself or others. Do it in the open when no one is around.

I will.

Mina turned and walked down the dune, returning to where Areg was. The elf raised his sword and shouted, "Ready more?"

She lifted her own sword in response, and the two clashed blades again. Gedrith's shadow passed over them as he left, and Mina hoped she would soon have another human around.

6

After two days of walking through woods and crossing over small rivers, the landscape subtly changed to flat plains. The tall grass swayed under a gentle breeze, but the wind did little to ease Caden's discomfort. There were no clouds in the sky, and the heat was unbearable despite the sun slowly creeping below the horizon. The occasional groupings of boulders cast long shadows that stretched along the field.

His feet ached from the effort, and his throat was dry. Droplets of sweat dripped down his face, and his stomach growled with hunger. He'd been strict with his rationing, perhaps too strict. He pushed on, driven by the thought of Lireth's captivity. Occasionally, he scanned the landscape, shielding his eyes against the sun's fading light with his right hand.

There was no sign of the dragons, but he spotted a glimmer that could be water. Caden changed direction, angling his steps northeast. A few minutes later, he saw the glimmer was indeed water, and he collapsed on his knees at the edge of the pool. Reaching his hands into the water, he splashed some onto his face, wiping the sweat and grime away.

It was a welcome relief, but he was starting to worry that he wasn't going in the right direction. He should have seen something by now. After drinking his fill, he replenished his leather waterskin with as much water as it would hold and stood, ready to continue his trek. A rustling among the reeds gave him pause, and he drew his sword. A small fox emerged. It regarded him with curiosity for a moment before scampering off.

Caden sheathed his blade and couldn't help smiling. The animal didn't count much for company, but its brief presence was a break from the monotony. He pulled some dried meat from his bag and devoured it, then continued his trek.

He walked until the stars were the only light in the sky before stopping to make camp. It took a lot of effort to keep his eyes open, and he fell asleep almost as soon as he lay down. When he opened his eyes, he was aware that he wasn't alone. A fire burned a few feet away, the flames banishing the cool night air.

Not daring to move, he tried to see who was tending the fire, but the figure was just out of his line of sight.

"I know you are awake," a soft voice said.

Caden sat up and rested his right hand on the hilt of his sword.

"Who are you?" he asked, his voice gruff from sleep.

The figure turned toward him, and the firelight revealed it was a woman. She was tall and lithe, with long dark hair and eyes that seemed to pull the light from the fire. She wore a simple tunic and pants, and a bow was slung across her back.

"I am the guardian of these lands," she said. "It has been a long time since I've seen another human out here."

"What do you want?" Caden tightened his grip on the hilt. Was she a ghost or something worse?

"I want nothing."

"Then why are you here?"

"Curiosity, I suppose. I saw you marching across the plains and decided to keep an eye on you. This area is inhospitable at best, and you looked like you could use some help."

Caden relaxed the grip on the hilt but kept his hand in place. He studied the woman for a moment, trying to gauge the truth of her intentions.

"I appreciate the offer, but I can take care of myself."

"What are you doing out here alone? Civilization is that way." She nodded back the way he'd come.

"I'm looking for something," Caden said vaguely.

"Care to share what that is? I may be able to point you in the right direction. I know these lands better than anyone."

Caden hesitated. He knew nothing about this woman, but she seemed genuine. He was getting nowhere on his own. If she turned out to be a threat, he would handle it.

"I'm searching for a group of dragons," he answered. "They would have passed this way about two weeks ago."

"I've seen them. They've taken up shelter in the mountains there." She pointed in the distance behind her. They were nothing more than a clump of shadows in the darkness, but Caden nodded. At least he had a clear direction now.

"I can lead you there, but it won't be easy."

"I don't need a guide," he said.

"You may not think so, but if I let you wander there on your own, you won't make it back."

Caden highly doubted that, but if she truly knew the area, then perhaps he should trust her enough to listen.

"Very well. Lead the way."

"First, we eat. I've got some rabbit left from my earlier catch. Then you need to rest. We'll leave at first light."

Caden was impatient to get moving, but he nodded and accepted a skewer from the woman.

"I'm Caden," he said.

"You can call me Eira."

They ate in silence for a moment, and then Eira began advising him of the dangers in the area. A band of soldiers from the Dracan Dominion had fled and setup camp at the base of the mountains. In desperation, they had turned to worshipping the dragons, offering things like gold and other humans in exchange for their lives.

Caden's stomach twisted at the thought. Instead of staying to ensure the safety of the commoners in the aftermath of the battle, they had fled like cowards and were offering their fellows to the dragons.

Despite his mistrust, he was glad to have someone to talk with. Something skittered in the darkness, and he snapped his gaze toward the sound.

"That's just Rem," Eira said.

Before Caden could ask who that was, the same fox he'd seen at the water pool earlier came trotting into view.

"Is that your pet?"

The fox stopped and glared at Caden, baring its teeth.

"Rem is no one's pet. He's my companion."

Caden rose his left brow in curiosity but said nothing. The fox curled up beside Eira and watched the wavering flames of the fire.

"Get some sleep," Eira told him. "I'll keep watch."

"Wake me when it's my turn."

"There's no need. I'll be fine."

"Suit yourself," Caden replied. He laid down

and eventually drifted back to sleep. When he awoke, it was still dark. He could see Eira's faint silhouette against the sky. She was sitting cross-legged in front of the fire. He was glad she hadn't merely been a dream.

"How long have I been asleep?" he asked, rubbing crud from his eyes as he got to his feet.

"Not long," Eira replied. "Just a few hours. Dawn is approaching."

Caden stretched and rubbed a sore spot on his neck. Sleeping on the ground wasn't very comfortable.

"I'm ready when you are."

Eira stood and brushed her pants off. She clicked her tongue, and Rem sprinted off toward the mountains. Caden looked at her questioningly, and she smiled.

"He's going to scout the way ahead."

Caden couldn't shake the feeling that there was something more to the fox. He had heard legends of people who could shapeshift into animals and wondered if Rem was truly a sorcerer in disguise.

"Come on," Eira said, interrupting his thoughts. "We've got a few hours before we reach the base."

Caden shrugged the thought away. As long as the two of them could lead him to the dragons, he didn't care what they were. Eira headed for the mountains, and he followed after her.

7

Mina saw little of Gedrith over the next few days, though she felt his constant presence through the bond. Her training was going well, but she tired of the same drills. She was also impatient to know the Enclave's answer.

She put on her armor and strapped her sword around her waist, then headed aboveground. It was early, and Areg had yet to rise. The sun was only a sliver on the horizon, but the sky was filled with colors that made her stop and pause to admire them. The temperature was cool and refreshing, but it wouldn't last. The Long Sands was an unforgiving place, full of heat, sand, and creatures that wanted to kill her.

Mina scanned the rest of the sky and saw a few dragons gliding upon the air currents. They were keeping watch for enemies. Despite no sand wyrm ever getting near the cave system, the dragons remained vigilant. She turned away and strode up the nearest dune. As she reached the top, a lizard darted away, startled by her presence.

She watched the creature until it was no longer visible, contemplating how it feared her while dragons feared nothing. The species were two heads of the same coin, at least in her estimation. Inhaling a deep breath, she closed her eyes and focused on the bond. She sensed Gedrith's fire and coaxed it through the bond until her throat grew warm. Parting her lips, she urged the fire forth.

Nothing happened.

She bid it a second time, and a third, all to no avail. Frustration turned to rage, and she clenched her hands into fists and screamed. The warmth in her throat faded, and she opened her eyes. Gedrith had told her it would take time to master the ability, but she didn't care. She wanted to do it *now*, not later.

You sound like a petulant child.

The voice startled her, and she opened her eyes to see the silver dragon who led the Enclave. How had she arrived without notice? Mina dropped to one knee and bowed her head.

Tiarna, she greeted.

The dragon regarded her in silence for a moment, and Mina wasn't sure if she should move or stay as she was.

Rise.

Mina lifted her head and slowly stood. *How can I be of service?*

Do you believe you are fit to be a dragon rider?

No.

Why not?

Mina paused. *I am not a warrior.*

The ways of war can be taught.

My past is filled with the blood of dragons.

We have forgiven you of those deeds.

Mina remained silent, not sure what else she could say.

The dragon looked out across the landscape. *It seems you struggle with the power you hold.*

Mina felt a pang of guilt wash over her. She was struggling, to the point that even the Enclave had noticed. How could she explain the turmoil inside her? She had lived a life of servitude, where her will was not her own. The bond with Gedrith had given her a newfound sense of power and freedom, but with those also came fear. The fear of losing it all and becoming a slave again.

I can sense your emotions. They are like chaos, swirling around one another, feeding the fear that makes you doubt yourself. You are the first human to speak with dragons in centuries, the first to bond with our kind since the Severance. You believe it happened by chance, but I do not. Whether you or I know the purpose, there is a reason you fell into that cave and landed on dragon scales.

Mina wanted to disagree, but she dared not interrupt the dragon. She cast her eyes to the ground, feeling as though she were being reprimanded like a child. And in a way, she was being scolded, but the dragon's words were a refining fire, burning away Mina's many excuses and revealing the strength underneath it all.

You are no longer a slave, Mina. Those days are

behind you. You are a dragon rider. Remove your doubts and be confident.

Thank you, Tiarna. Your kind words have helped me more than you know.

Good.

The two were silent for a moment, both staring out at the rolling hills of sand. Mina cleared her throat and looked at the dragon from her periphery.

Did Gedrith ... ask anything of the Enclave?

He did.

Mina waited impatiently, anxiously curling and uncurling her toes. There was sand in her boots, and the grit rubbed the skin between the cracks of her toes.

Has the Enclave decided?

The dragon looked at her, meeting her gaze. *We have decided we will not allow another human into our domain.*

I understand. She tried her best to hide her disappointment, but it must have been evident on her face.

Take heart. It is not for the reasons you likely think. We are not cruel, nor do we seek to be. The world is hardly ready for the return of dragons, much less dragon riders. That endeavor will take time.

Everything takes time, Mina complained.

It is the way of the world, as you know. A babe

does not come into the world fully formed.

How will people come to accept dragons if you do not show yourself to them?

That is something the Enclave has considered. I believe the answer lies with you.

Me? What do you mean?

It will take years of training with Areg for you to be ready to go into the world, but if we want to ensure another Lord D'Lance does not arise, we cannot wait that long. We have decided that you and Gedrith will be sent out to patrol the dominions and provide aid where you can. As people come to see your deeds, you will gain their trust. That is the first of many steps that will allow us to return without meeting violence and confusion.

Mina repeated the words in her mind, surprised to hear them. *You think I am ready for that?*

Are you not?

Pushing her doubts and fears aside, she bowed her head. *I am. Thank you for putting your trust in me. I will do my best to prepare the world for the truth about dragons.*

I trust you will. There is another matter you must know, as it is something you will need to deal with.

What is it?

The one bound to Lireth escaped his prison.

Caden. Mina's heart leaped in her chest. *How?* she asked.

It was the draman. They've been regrouping since the battle at Velbridge, and now they have their leader back.

They're going to come for her, Mina said, a statement more than a question. She looked over her shoulder at the cave entrance.

So long as their bond exists, nothing will stop him from seeking her.

Mina knew what needed to be done. She'd always known whether she wanted to admit it to herself or not.

I will take care of it.

Be wary. Lireth's corruption knows no limits, and he will do whatever he must to eliminate obstacles in his path. The person you once knew is gone.

Yes, Tiarna. When do you want us to leave?

I will give you three days to prepare. Take anything you need.

Thank you. Mina knelt and bowed her head. *Tiarna.*

You have earned the right to call me by name. It is Silvara.

With that, Silvara stretched her wings and leaped into the air, returning to the cave. Mina remained where she was, her thoughts a whirlwind. She should have felt more honored to be given the right to call Silvara by her name, but she was too troubled by the other news.

Caden had escaped.

8

Eira led the way across the plains, and as they reached the foothills of the mountains, the grass faded to more rocky terrain. The air was dusty, and Caden fought the impulse to frequently drink from his waterskin, knowing he needed to conserve his meager supply.

"Do you see the cave there?"

Caden squinted up at the mountain, trying to make out the details.

"That's where the dragons are," Eira said grimly. "We'll have to climb up there to get to them."

"We?"

"You didn't plan on going up there alone, did you? Aside from the climb, you'll also have to deal with the rogue soldiers. And, of course, the dragons themselves."

"I'll be fine," Caden said, though he wondered if the dragons were as loyal to Lireth as he was. If not, he probably wouldn't get far before they flamed him. As he considered it further, he decided to let the woman come with him. At the very worst, he could use her as a diversion to escape. "But you can come if you'd like."

"I don't have anything else to do out here, so why not?" She grinned at him.

"Aren't you afraid of the dragons?"

Eira shrugged. "I'm afraid of many things, but fear is nothing more than an emotion that needs to be controlled. Do you need to rest before we start?"

Caden was tired, but he didn't want to waste time. He shook his head and steeled himself for the climb, reminding himself that Lireth was likely in more dire conditions. They began their ascent. The rocks were jagged and unforgiving, and one misstep could mean a deadly fall. Caden struggled clumsily, but Eira's steps were sure and steady. He strove to keep up with her swift pace, refusing to fall behind.

"You're quite skilled at this," he huffed, baffled at how she seemed to glide up the mountain.

"I'm used to it," she called back, not even winded.

Finally, they reached a plateau just below the cave entrance. Eira put a dust-covered finger to her lips and motioned with her other hand. Voices drifted in the air, and Caden pressed his back against the mountain, glad for a break. His muscles ached, and he was parched. He drank sparingly from the waterskin, consuming just enough to rid the dust from his throat. He offered the skin to Eira, but she shook her head.

Rem skittered onto the ledge, and Eira knelt and scratched his head. She leaned in close and whispered something to the fox that Caden didn't hear, and the creature scrambled up to the ledge where the cave was. They waited in silence, and Caden stared at the vast plains that stretched out into the distance. He could see the pool of water he'd come across the day before and wished it were closer. He wanted nothing more than to dunk himself beneath its cool surface.

The fox returned, leaping down onto the plateau. It barked and yipped excitedly. Eira shushed him and scratched his head again, then looked at Caden and whispered, "Rem says there are six men up there, all of them armed. The dragons are sleeping."

Caden stared at Eira for a moment, trying to comprehend what she said. "That thing can talk?"

"All animals can talk. It's a matter of whether you're listening."

Again, he suspected magic was involved with these two, but that would be useful if things went badly with the soldiers. He shrugged in reply and started to climb up to the next ledge. Eira grabbed his leg and pulled him back down.

"We can't just rush in there," she said. "There may be traps."

"What do you propose?"

Eira smiled. "An ambush. We'll wait until they come out of the cave and catch them off guard."

Caden decided that was a better idea than trying to fight them in the darkness of the cavern. And if the dragons heard the sound of fighting, he may not have the opportunity to explain why he was there before they joined the fray.

"We'll need to give them a reason to come out here," he said.

"Rem can manage that, can't you, Rem?"

The fox chittered and brushed up against Eira, much like a dog.

"I take it he said yes?"

"And just a moment ago, you didn't think animals could speak. You're a quick learner."

Caden snorted and shook his head. "I'd rather be up there when they come out. Maybe we can hide among the rocks."

"Good idea."

They climbed up onto the ledge, and Caden hid behind a cluster of rocks on the left. Eira sprinted across the rock shelf and climbed up the face of the mountain to the right of the cave, taking a position above the entrance. She unslung her bow and nocked an arrow. Caden unsheathed his sword and tilted his neck to either side until it popped, then loosened his shoulders. He gave Eira a nod, and Rem ran into the cave.

Caden held his breath and waited. A commotion echoed out of the cave, and Rem sprinted into view, leaping over the ledge and disappearing. Caden adjusted his grip on the hilt of his sword as a tall brute of a man stepped out, carrying a large ax. Before Caden could engage him, Eira fired her arrow, striking the man in the back. His chest thrust forward from the momentum, and he staggered a few steps before tripping. He fell over the ledge, crashing to the plateau below. All went still, and for a moment, Caden thought the other soldiers weren't coming.

"Jon! Where'd ye go?"

A second soldier, this one shorter than the first, strode out of the cave, looking left and right. Caden looked at Eira, who nodded at him, signaling this one was his. He stepped out from behind the boulders and rushed the man, his sword flashing in the sunlight.

The man barely had time to draw his sword, but he brought it up in time to block Caden's strike. The clang of their steel echoed off the mountainside, and the alarmed shouts of the other soldiers joined the cacophony.

Caden feinted left and struck right, but the soldier parried the blow. He followed up with a kick to the knee, and the soldier stumbled. Seizing the opportunity, Caden aimed for the thin line between the man's armor and plunged his sword into the soldier's chest. The remaining soldiers emerged from the cave, temporarily startled by the scene.

An arrow struck one of them in the head, splattering the others with blood. Before Caden could engage another foe, Eira dispatched the rest of them with deadly accuracy, her arrows *whizzing* as they sailed through the air. With the thrill of battle ended, Caden wiped his sword on one of the bodies and sheathed it, then looked at the faces of the men. They wore Lord D'Lance's emblem, but they weren't Runesmen.

"That was easy enough," Eira said, joining him. "Look at their eyes, though. They look …"

"Sick?" Caden offered. "I thought so, too. At first, I thought it was the look of madness, but this is something else."

Caden looked at the cave entrance with renewed concern.

9

Since she was leaving soon, Areg gave Mina the day off from training. He helped her pack supplies for the journey, and afterward, gifted her with a thick traveling cloak. She tried to refuse, but the elf wouldn't budge on the matter.

With nothing else to take up her time, she wandered to the chamber that held Lireth. The dragon wasn't pacing this time. Instead, she was curled up on the floor. Mina peered through the glass wall and the two locked eyes.

The smell of rose and orchid filled the air, and Mina knew beyond any doubt that Lireth was well aware of what was happening beyond her prison.

"You know they are coming for you, don't you?" she whispered to herself.

This place will burn, Lireth said, invading Mina's mind. She gasped in surprise and pushed the dragon away, forcing a mental wall up. Lireth rumbled heartily, then glowered as Gedrith sped through the hall to Mina's side.

Your draman will never make it through the desert, Gedrith replied, allowing Mina to hear his response. *And if they do, we will crush them like ants.*

We shall see, Lireth growled.

Indeed, we shall.

The two dragons glared at each other for a moment before Lireth turned her back to the cave wall.

Come with me, Gedrith told Mina.

He led her through the tunnels until they came to an area Mina had not seen before. Unlike the rest of the place, this chamber wasn't illuminated brightly. Gedrith paused at the threshold to swivel his head in her direction.

I can see well enough, she said.

He stepped into the cavern and Mina followed, her eyes slowly adjusting to the gloom. Once they did, she stiffened in astonishment. A literal hill of coins rose from the ground. Gold, silver, bronze … Mina guessed the value of it all was enough to rival even the High Price's wealth.

Take what you need for our journey.

Where did all this come from?

All across the dominions.

Mina had seen the spoils of Lord Klodian's hunts before, but this was hard to wrap her mind around.

There's something I've always been curious about. Why do dragons hoard money?

It has no value to us, Gedrith said. *Not in the ways it does to humans. We have it for more practical reasons.*

What do you mean?

When we are still in our eggs, our scales have no color. We are translucent by nature. These coins are mined from minerals within the earth, and those minerals give us our color. The larger the hoard, the more powerful a dragon is when it hatches.

Mina frowned. *I don't understand. There are all different coins here. How would a dragon's scales only be one color?*

Gedrith chuckled. *We are naturally drawn to one specific mineral. Though there may be different metals present, only the one we are attuned to affects our color. It is a mystery we ourselves have yet to unravel.*

What about the other dragons? The chromatic ones like Lireth?

They are drawn to gemstones instead of metals. Lireth was probably partial to onyx or obsidian.

Do only females hoard treasure?

No. Males will also do so when they are ready for a mate.

What metal gave you your color?

Copper, Gedrith replied. It was the same name he had given her when they first met. She found that funny.

Mina walked to the pile of coins and grabbed a handful. She held them up for inspection. Various inscriptions were on all of them. She recognized a few from the Thophate Dominion, and one from the Dracan, but the others were foreign to her. The coins clinked as she put them into her coin purse.

Is that enough?

More than enough, she replied, casting a look around the cavern. *Are there eggs in here?*

There are.

Gedrith drew near and used a claw to gently move some coins aside, uncovering an enormous egg. It was very different from the one she had taken from Lord Klodian.

Can I touch it?

Gedrith was silent for a moment, and she thought he would refuse. Finally, he lowered his head and nudged it out of the coins. Mina reached out and laid a hand on the egg. A steady pulse beat against the shell, and her eyes widened. She was amazed and humbled all at once, and tears stung her eyes.

This is amazing, she said. She ran her hand along the shell, feeling the many grooves and their hard texture. *How long before a dragon hatches?*

That depends on the dragon. Every hatchling is different.

Mina couldn't help but feel a sense of awe as she gazed upon the egg. She wondered what kind of dragon would emerge and what its fate would be. Would it be like Lireth, evil and imprisoned for eternity? Or would it be noble like Gedrith, free to roam the skies?

We should leave now, Gedrith said. *The eggs*

should remain undisturbed.

Mina nodded and reluctantly removed her hand from the egg. She watched as Gedrith nestled it back into place, then scooped up a claw full of coins and reburied it.

Are dragons born already knowing their purpose in life, or do they have to discover it like humans? And is their purpose a matter of choice, or are they bound by fate?

Gedrith laughed softly, the sound echoing off the cave walls. *We are born with an innate knowledge of some things, but our fates are our own to decide.*

What about being bound to me? That wasn't a choice on your end. It was more a coincidence than anything. It's possible that could be the workings of fate, couldn't it?

Gedrith remained silent for a moment. *Perhaps. You have given me something to consider. Come.*

She followed him out of the cave and parted ways with him, returning to her chamber. Everything she planned on taking was packed aside from the cloak Areg had given her, and she rolled it up and set it next to her pack. A faint rustling sound caught her attention, and she turned to see the elf standing near the entryway.

"It nice. Know you."

"The honor is mine," Mina replied. "You've taught me so much. I'm indebted to you."

"No debt. Do good. That repay."

"I will do my best."

Mina approached him and knelt, becoming eye level with the elf. "You are a great warrior," she said. "I hope I do not offend you, but may I give you a hug?"

A grin spread across Areg's lips and he wrapped his arms around her, squeezing her tightly. He was stronger than he looked, and she returned the embrace.

"Thank you for everything."

"No leave. Eat first."

"Eat?"

"Feast. Enclave give honor."

"To who?

"You."

10

"Can dragons control people? That doesn't seem possible. They're just wild animals."

Caden considered sparing her the harsh reality, but he decided it wouldn't do her any good to believe that. They would eventually part ways, and after Lireth destroyed the Enclave, all of humanity might be her next target. It was better to give her a chance at survival. At least, that's what his conscience told him.

"Dragons are far more than wild animals. Unlike your fox friend here, they can do much more than speak."

Eira's face scrunched in confusion. "What do you mean?"

"It's too much to explain, but they are sentient creatures, more powerful than we know."

"So they *can* control people?"

Caden thought about his bond with Lireth. Had she taken over his will and controlled him? He didn't think so, but …

"That may be possible," he said. "I don't know for certain."

"Then we must kill them."

"No."

"Why not?"

"It would take a Dominion Lord with the power of many Runesmen to kill a single dragon. I'm certain there is more than one in there, and even if we could kill them, I don't want to. I need their help."

Eira stared at him curiously, waiting for an explanation.

"It's a complicated story, and one I do not care to tell. We can part ways now if you'd like. I understand if you don't want to involve yourself." Caden looked at the dead soldiers. "I appreciate your help with this lot either way."

"I have many questions, but I know when it is best not to pry." She paused. "I will see this task through with you, if for nothing else than to satisfy my curiosity."

Caden chuckled. "Very well. If things don't go as planned, flee. I don't need a hero trying to save my skin."

Eira bowed her head, but she said nothing. Caden didn't force the matter. If she wanted to face certain death, it was her choice. Sheathing his sword, Caden wiped the sweat that had collected on his forehead with the back of his hand and stepped into the cave.

The air was cool and damp, a welcome reprieve from the growing heat outside. He stepped lightly, careful not to kick any loose rocks. Eira was as stealthy as Rem, and he had to glance over his shoulder to make sure she was following him.

The darkness became all-consuming, and Caden had to feel along the wall to know where he was going. Eira tapped him on the shoulder, halting his steps.

"Rem can guide us," she whispered.

"Please," he replied, glad for the help. Walking blind was likely to get them killed, especially if they unknowingly stumbled into the dragons. He felt the fox brush against his leg as it took the lead, but he realized they still had the same problem. Rem could see in the dark, but they couldn't.

As if answering his unspoken concern, a faint green light illuminated the tunnel. Rem looked back, and Caden saw the light shining from the fox's eyes. His heart thumped in his chest at the eerie spectacle, but Rem turned his gaze ahead and trotted onward silently.

There was no denying the fox was a magical creature now. He was glad to have them as allies. The tunnel stretched for a few hundred feet before sloping downward and opening into a massive chamber. Rem's eyes abruptly stopped glowing, and before Caden could question why, he heard a hissing noise that echoed off the cavern walls.

Instinctively, his hand went to the hilt of his sword, but he knew it was foolish. The blade was useless against such creatures. He took a single step, and the sound stopped. He clenched his jaw, preparing for the worst.

I can smell you, a voice penetrated his mind. It overwhelmed his senses, nowhere near as controlled as Lireth's voice.

Then you must recognize my scent.

There was only silence, so he continued.

I am here on behalf of Lireth. The Enclave took her captive, and I seek your help in freeing her.

He heard multiple forms moving around in the darkness, and he fought the urge to turn and run.

If Lireth was weak enough to be captured, then she deserves her fate with the Enclave. Be gone, human, before I make you nothing more than a pile of ash.

Caden was afraid they might refuse. He needed to instill the level of fear that Lireth did, but how was he to do that when he wasn't a threat to them? Something tickled the edge of his senses. It was faint, so he knew it wasn't the dragon. Closing his eyes, he reached out with his mind. Like a bolt of lightning, he felt Lireth's presence invade his being.

"Fools!" she hissed through his mouth. "You will come to The Long Sands with my army, or you shall know my wrath!"

Just as quickly as she had come, she was gone. Caden dropped to his knees, overcome with weakness. The runes on his neck burned, and he reached back, rubbing at them feebly with his right hand. He tried to connect to her through the bond, but just as before, there was nothing but an empty abyss at the other end. Although he couldn't sense her, she knew what was happening around him.

Eira tucked her hand under his armpit and helped him back to his feet. The weakness faded, and the trembling left his knees. Taking a deep breath, he spoke aloud.

"You have heard the command of our master. Decide for yourself what you will do. You can find us in the same place we were before the battle at Velbridge, but it would not be wise to be seen. The High Prince has his men patrolling the area, and we don't need more problems than we already have. Meet us at the edge of the Dracan Dominion and be prepared to fight. The Enclave will not give Lireth up willingly."

Caden waited a moment to see if the dragons would respond, but they said nothing.

"Take us out of here," he said to Rem, hoping the fox would do as he asked. The green glow from the creature's eyes flooded the cavern, and Caden saw three black dragons staring at him. Rem scurried down the tunnel, and the darkness returned. Satisfied he had done all he could, Caden turned and followed Rem and Eira back out to the ledge.

They emerged from the cave, and Caden blinked against the sunlight. Eira stood at his side, but he found it impossible to read her expression. Rem watched him curiously, his head cocked to one side.

"I guess this is where we part ways," he said, looking out across the landscape. It was a long walk to the camp, and despite his exhaustion, he was eager to head back.

"I'm not sure what transpired back there, but I'm too invested to leave now. I'm coming with you. If you'll have me, that is."

Rem yipped, and Eira smiled. "If you'll have *us*."

"It will be dangerous," he warned.

"I've never been one to back down from a challenge."

"You will see things that have no explanation … odd things."

"Good. We should get going if we want to make good progress before making camp."

Caden watched Eira climb down the ledge. She remained a mystery for now, but all things would be revealed in time. He started down the mountain, determination guiding his steps.

Lireth was still with him, even if he couldn't feel her presence.

11

The next day, Mina was slow to rise. She'd eaten too much and was tired from having stayed up so late. Though dragons didn't consume alcohol, they could certainly host a grand affair. She groaned as she slipped on her boots. Wiping the sleep from her eyes, she noticed Areg was waiting near the entryway of her chamber.

"Sleep long," he said, a grin pulling at his lips.

"How are you so happy in the morning?"

The elf shrugged. "Natural."

Mina wished she had as much energy as he did. She stifled a yawn and belted on her sword, then grabbed her pack from beside her bed. Casting a glance around the room, she decided she was ready. While she was excited to be back among humans, she was nervous. What if the world didn't accept dragons as they once did?

You're awake, Gedrith's voice interrupted her thoughts. *Good. Come up here. We need to go.*

Mina sensed something pressing behind his words. *Sand wyrm?*

I'll explain on the way.

"What's going on out there?" she asked Areg.

"Draman march."

Mina hurried past the elf and rushed through the tunnels. Gedrith was waiting for her at the top of the sloped entrance. The sun was already high in the sky, and she blinked against the brightness. She strapped her pack across her shoulder and climbed onto his back. Before she could say anything, Gedrith leaped into the air. He flapped his mighty wings, rising higher and higher, then turned west.

Areg said the draman are marching. Are they coming this way? Mina asked.

We are not sure, but it would be foolish not to assume as much.

How close are they?

A few days away. Their progress is slow, but they are traveling east. We must stop them before they enter the desert.

Are more dragons coming to help?

No.

How will we stop them on our own?

We must remove the one that guides them. With him gone, the draman should lose the desire to free Lireth.

Caden. The image of him chained to the wall in Lord Culver's dungeon was seared into her mind's eye. She hadn't expected him to escape, but she also hadn't counted on the draman to regroup. Imprisoning him again wasn't the answer. She knew that, though she didn't want to admit it. He would have to die. That was the only way to sever his bond with Lireth. She steeled her heart, knowing if Gedrith didn't kill him with fire, she would have to do it with her blade. Mina's stomach churned with unease. She didn't want to kill him, but she knew it was necessary.

As they flew, she looked down at the landscape. They passed over blue rivers and green forests, but her mind was elsewhere. She was thinking of Caden, of the friendship he had offered her when they first met. He'd willingly put himself in harm's way to defend her from Thais. Mina smiled at the memory, temporarily forgetting what was to come.

As the distance passed, Mina's exhaustion grew. She laid against Gedrith's neck and closed her eyes, thinking only to rest them a moment. Darkness overtook her, but she jolted awake when she experienced the sensation of falling. She was relieved to find she was still safely on Gedrith's back, though the scenery below had changed.

Where are we? she asked.

We are approaching the Dracan Dominion.

Already?

You've been asleep for a while now.

Mina sat up and stretched her neck, feeling a kink in it. The wind whipped her hair about, and she pushed the strands aside and stared down at the ground. They were flying over farmland, and the tracts of various colors stood out among the surrounding landscape. She didn't see any signs of the draman, however.

Do you know where they are?

They should be in the woods outside Velbridge.

Gedrith sped up, and the wind buffeted Mina. She held on tightly to Gedrith's neck scales and kept her head down to protect her eyes. She remained in that position until he slowed his pace, then lifted her head to see where they were.

The ruined city of Velbridge stretched out below them. It was a sight both awe-inspiring and heart-wrenching. The once great city was now a shadow of its former glory. The buildings were empty shells, crumbled and charred, while the streets were littered with debris and ash. There was no sign of movement, and Mina knew the living had abandoned the place.

The fires must have burned the entire city down, she said. *Where did all the people go? This was the home of thousands.*

They are scattered to the wind, I am sure. There is no sense in staying in a place like this.

Gedrith landed near the center of the city, and Mina climbed down his shoulder to stand amid the rubble. Nothing was recognizable. She couldn't even pinpoint where she had killed Lord D'Lance.

I smell them, Gedrith rumbled.

Mina scanned the rubble, but there was no movement nor any sign of life.

Let's search them out, Mina said.

The two crossed over mounds of rubble,

traveling east toward the forest. Ash covered everything, and by the time they reached the scorched wall, Mina's boots were stained black with soot. She stepped through a ruined entryway, the gate completely missing. Even the hinges were gone. Gedrith leaped over the wall, his trail smacking the upper stones. A few of them fell, clattering to the ground.

They trudged across a short, barren field and entered the forest. The outer edge of trees was dead, their leaves gone and their trunks blackened. Mina couldn't believe how far the devastation stretched, but as they moved deeper into the forest, signs of life returned.

The smell of burning wood reached Mina's nostrils, and she drew her sword. She turned to Gedrith and motioned for him to stay where he was. The trees ahead were thicker, and he would have trouble getting through without making too much noise.

I'll scout ahead, she told him.

Gedrith remained silent, and she stalked onward as quietly as she could manage. Voices drifted in the air, and she peered through the brush and saw a clearing. A group of draman was gathered around a campfire. A short distance away from them was another group, and another. Mina's eyes darted from one to the next, quickly realizing there were dozens of the creatures, if not hundreds.

There are many draman here.

Do not concern yourself with them. Look for the

human that leads them.

Mina scanned the encampment, but she didn't see Caden anywhere. She crept closer, squinting at the groups further away. Perhaps the only good thing about there being so many draman was there would be no mistaking Caden among them. The draman near the campfire were talking, but she couldn't make out what they were saying. She inched toward the clearing, her heart pounding wildly.

The splintering sound of a twig breaking under her boot made her halt in place. She swallowed hard and waited. The draman didn't seem to notice the noise. She exhaled in relief and took one step before something heavy slammed into her from behind, sending her sprawling to the ground. Leaves and grit smothered her face, and Mina quickly scrambled to her feet, searching for her sword.

A draman towered over her, his scales glistening as if polished. The creature bared its fangs at her, and she snatched up her blade and took a step back. She brought the sword up and took a defensive stance, but she knew she was in trouble. The scores of draman behind her were quickly approaching, but she dared not risk a glance over her shoulder.

The ground trembled, sending vibrations up her calves. The draman who'd knocked her over looked around, his reptilian face wrinkling in what she assumed was confusion. Gedrith burst through the trees, his massive claw crushing the draman with hardly any effort.

Sorry, she said, whirling around to face the oncoming hoard. *I didn't see that one.*

Gedrith issued a deafening roar and stormed ahead. Tightening her grip on the hilt of her blade, Mina ran after him.

12

The journey back to the camp took less time than Caden's foray into the wilderness, mainly because Eira took the lead. She knew the landscape better than he did, and Caden realized he'd originally taken a much longer route. They'd arrived late in the night, and to his surprise, she didn't seem taken aback by the presence of the draman. Bast gave her a tent, which she shared with Rem, and Caden tiredly collapsed in his own pavilion.

He slept without dreaming, and when he opened his eyes, he realized something had awakened him. The clash of steel, cries of pain, and the roar of a dragon. Caden sprang up from his bedroll and hurriedly put his boots and armor on, then scrambled out of his tent, looking to the sky.

It was difficult to see anything beyond the canopy of the forest, but there didn't seem to be any dragons overhead. Several draman rushed past him, heading toward the ruins of Velbridge.

"What's going on?" he shouted.

"We're under attack!"

Caden cursed and followed them, drawing his sword. As he drew nearer to the battle, he spotted an enormous red dragon. Why was a dragon attacking them? Was it rebelling against Lireth's command to aid her army?

And then he saw a human, a woman, clashing swords with a draman. Her blonde hair whipped about as she spun and twisted. His heart skipped a beat.

It was Mina.

A surge of conflicting emotions overtook him. Part of him was relieved to see she was alive and well, and the other part… well, he wanted to make her pay for leaving him to rot in a dungeon. He watched her fight, impressed with her sword skill. She'd clearly been training.

Mina parried the draman's strike, forcing his blade out wide, then stepped forward and rammed the hilt of her blade into the draman's snout. The creature stumbled back from the blow but didn't cry out in pain. Draman were made of tougher stuff than humans, a fact Caden continued to admire.

He continued to watch her for a moment longer, then shouted her name. All eyes turned to him, including hers. She briefly stiffened, but it was long enough that he noticed the reaction. Was it surprise … or fear?

Caden didn't have time to dwell on it, as Mina's dragon met his gaze. Raising his sword, he issued a battle cry and rushed forward. The dragon flapped his wings, and a powerful gust of wind sent the nearby draman tumbling backward. Too far away to be affected, Caden slowed his pace and changed direction, heading for Mina instead.

He was only a few feet away when her dragon let out a deafening roar that shook the ground beneath his feet. Mina didn't flinch. She swung her sword in a fluid motion and came at him. Caden dodged the attack and retaliated with a swift strike of his own. The clang of metal echoed off the trees as their blades met.

"What are you doing here?" he demanded.

"I should ask you the same thing," Mina replied. "You're supposed to be in Lord Culver's dungeon."

He could see it in her eyes. The fear. And it only fueled his anger. How dare she leave him in that cell? She'd betrayed him, and he couldn't forgive her for that. Her words came back to him.

Our destinies may be entwined, but they are not united.

She was right. Although he cared for her, he knew his feelings were deceiving. Their paths were too different, their goals at odds with one another.

"I'm sorry," he said.

Her expression morphed from anger to confusion, and she backed away a few steps. That was all he needed. With her guard down, he lunged forward, the tip of his sword aimed at her throat. Mina deftly sidestepped the strike, and he realized her confusion was merely an act. She came at him again, and Caden parried the attack.

"Why are you doing this?" she asked. "Why do you still follow Lireth after all she's done?"

"You betrayed me," Caden said.

"*I* betrayed *you?* You're the one who's gone

down a dark path. Your dragon is evil, Caden! How do you not see that?"

They circled each other, both wary. Caden thought he had more experience with a blade than she did, but whoever had trained her did their job well. They matched each other evenly, and he knew the only way to win would be to disarm her. From his periphery, he could see her dragon was fighting a swarm of draman. He needed to end this quickly, before the beast slaughtered his men and killed him next.

Caden feinted a thrust, then swung his sword to the right, hoping to catch her off guard. Mina twirled aside, seeing through his trick. They exchanged blows, neither one gaining the advantage.

"Surrender," Mina huffed. Droplets of sweat rolled down her face.

"No."

"You'll never win, Caden. You're fighting for the wrong side."

"You're wrong about that. Stop trying to sway me. We have chosen our paths, and I intend to see mine through to the end."

Caden's muscles burned from the strain of his efforts. Fatigue was overtaking him, and he wasn't sure how much longer he could continue the fight. His forces easily outnumbered Mina and her dragon, but there was nothing that could defeat a dragon. At least, nothing at Caden's disposal.

Mina lunged at him, breaking his reverie. He blocked her strike, but there was an unnatural power behind her blow, and her sword shattered his to pieces. Caden stared dumbfounded at the broken blade in his hands. Mina wasn't a Runesman, so where had her strength come from? She leveled her sword at his throat. He looked up at her and could see the triumph in her eyes.

"It's over," she said. "You've lost."

A multitude of roars filled the air, and Caden saw Mina's eyes flick upward. The confidence in her expression faded. He slapped the flat of her blade, pushing it away from his neck, and tried to wrestle the sword from her grasp. Mina fought back, and for an intense moment, they were locked in an unwinnable struggle. With that same unnatural strength, Mina twisted the blade out of his grip and kicked him in the chest, sending him sprawling backward.

She turned and fled to her dragon, quickly climbing up his side. Caden scrambled onto his feet and turned to look toward the roars. Several black dragons, the ones from the mountain cave, were approaching the forest. Bast and a group of draman encircled him, forming a protective ring.

"They decided to come," Bast said.

"Lireth's wrath knows no bounds," Caden replied. "They feared what would happen if they did not obey her."

He turned back to look at Mina and saw she and her dragon had already fled.

"Should we pursue them, my lord?"

Caden stared into the distance for a moment.

"No," he answered, deciding to let her get away for now.

Her death would be much sweeter with Lireth watching.

13

I had him! We need to go back!

Gedrith didn't respond. He continued flying east, away from the enemy.

Turn around!

Do not be foolish, Gedrith chided. *We could not have won. Not after those dragons arrived. They are as vicious and cruel as Lireth, and I can only do so much.*

Caden lost. I had him.

And yet you did not kill him when you had the opportunity. You hesitated.

Mina's anger deflated. She knew he was right. She had indeed held back. A part of her still cared for him, despite everything that had happened. But she couldn't let that cloud her judgment. He had made his choice, and even affirmed it. It was now her duty to stop him.

Where are we going? she asked, trying to distract herself from her thoughts.

Gedrith descended, landing in an open field.

We wait.

Wait?

We will wait and watch their movements. If they march toward The Long Sands, we will strike when the time is right.

What if we do not get a chance to strike at them?

Gedrith rumbled and pulled his wings against his body. *Then we will fight them in the desert.*

Mina dismounted and sat down on the grass, leaning her back against Gedrith's side. She closed her eyes and inhaled a deep breath. The battle had taken a toll on her, both physically and emotionally. Caden had almost fallen to her blade, but her emotions had once again thwarted her. She couldn't let her feelings get in the way of her duty. Not again. The steady rise and fall of Gedrith's body eased her mind, and she pushed the tumultuous thoughts aside.

The hours dragged on, and eventually, the sun set beyond the horizon. Mina had caught a rabbit, and it was cooking over a small fire Gedrith had made for her. She'd flattened the grass around the fire and ringed it with stones to keep it from spreading and burning the entire field. The sky was cloudless, and the moon shone brightly, providing plenty of light.

It was just as she was dozing off beside the fire that she heard it. The marching of soldiers. Mina's eyes snapped open, and she rose to her feet, her right hand grabbing the hilt of her sword. She looked at Gedrith. The dragon was asleep. Mina roused him by prodding his shoulder with her blade. He opened his eyes, and they reflected the moonlight, reminding her of a stray cat she'd once seen. They both turned their gaze toward the noise.

In the distance, torches flickered, and the rhythmic sound of boots hitting the ground grew steadily louder.

That can't be the draman, can it?

Gedrith silently stared into the distance for a moment, then turned his head to regard her. *It is them.*

Mina knew they were not ordinary men, but the distance they had traveled seemed an impossible feat. She had clearly underestimated them.

If the main force is this close, the dragons aren't far off, Gedrith said. *We must be wary.*

An idea came to Mina then, though she didn't know the likelihood of success.

If we can get close enough to find Caden, I can try to hit him with an arrow.

I do not think it is worth the risk.

You said yourself that if we cut the head from the enemy, the others will lose their desire.

I'm aware of my words, but even dragons can be wrong. And how will you hit him with an arrow? You do not have a bow.

Not yet, she replied. *If the main force is here, then I'm certain there are scouts nearby. I can take one of theirs.*

Do not grow smug in your abilities. Conceit is the downfall of many.

I'm not smug. I had good mentors who taught me much.

Flattery will not change my mind.

It was worth a try, Mina said, smiling at the dragon.

While I do not like the risk, the draman will be devastated if we can kill Lireth's puppet. Go and find a bow. I will remain here until you are ready.

Without any hesitation, Mina sprinted off. She would rather have Gedrith at her side, especially since she couldn't see as well as him in the dark, but it was probably better he stayed where he was. It would be hard to miss a dragon stalking about, and if he took to the skies, the other dragons would see him.

She ran toward the army, her sword pointed behind her. As she drew nearer, she could hear the deep, guttural voices of the draman. They marched in a loose formation, seeming unconcerned about potential enemies. Mina kept a safe distance, moving among the shadows as much as possible to keep herself hidden. She searched for a lone scout, one isolated from the main group.

It took some time, but she finally spotted one. He was walking on the outskirts of the formation, oblivious to her approach. The silhouette of a bow stretched across his shoulders. She thought it an odd way to carry a bow, but she had her target. She stepped lightly, her heart racing. Once she was within striking distance, she held her breath and aimed, then jabbed her sword forward with all her strength. The tip of her blade struck the draman between the scales on the back of his neck before slicing through his flesh.

The creature stumbled and collapsed with a wet gurgle. Mina pulled her sword free and looked around, making sure there were no other scouts. The army had halted its advance, but nothing seemed to be amiss. She knelt and grabbed the bow, only to realize it was actually a crossbow. She groaned but took the weapon anyway. It was one she had not trained with before, but it would have to do.

Glancing in the direction of the army again, she noticed they were setting up tents. It seemed even draman needed a break. She sprinted back to where Gedrith was and paused to catch her breath.

I found a crossbow, but there's only one bolt for it. There's something on the tip, too.

Let me see it, Gedrith said.

Mina removed the quarrel and held it up. The dragon sniffed the air near the tip of the projectile.

It's poison.

That should do the job. I just need to get near enough to hit him without getting caught.

We will fly over the camp.

What about the dragons? What if they see us?

We will be quick. Whether your aim is true or not, we will make one pass and then we shall return to the Enclave. They need to know what's coming.

Mina put the bolt back in place and stared at the

weapon for a moment in silence. She had one chance to strike Caden. If she missed, then she knew killing him would have to be more direct. Issuing a plea to Avera, she strapped the crossbow over her shoulder and climbed onto Gedrith's back.

I've not used one of these. How does it compare to a bow? she asked.

It is more accurate, but it doesn't require the strength a bow does. I will fly as low as I can, but you will need to adjust how you aim.

Gedrith sent an image of Lucius, his previous rider, through the bond. Mina thought it looked easier than using a bow. She grabbed the crossbow and set it in her lap, holding it in place with her left hand while gripping Gedrith with her right.

I'm ready.

Gedrith stretched his wings out and leaped into the sky. The cool night air whipped around Mina, and she shivered as a chill ran down her back. The glow of campfires came into view, and she squeezed her knees tightly against Gedrith's sides and lifted the crossbow with both hands. As they reached the camp, Gedrith glided on the currents, flying little more than a dozen feet above the tents. Mina scanned the area, looking for Caden.

There, Gedrith said, sending the image to her. He was standing next to a draman, one she had seen before. The dragon changed direction, taking her straight toward him. She positioned the crossbow and aimed at him.

Time seemed to stand still. Her pulse pounded in her ears, overpowering the sound of the wind. Caden pointed at something, his lips moving with a command she couldn't hear. A wave of heat washed over her as she remembered their kiss. It had been so unexpected, but his lips had been soft and warm.

Focus.

Gedrith's voice broke her reverie. She closed one eye and centered her aim. Her finger tightened on the trigger, and her breath caught in her throat. It took everything she had to will herself to pull it.

Three, two, one…

Mina squeezed the trigger. The string twanged, and the bolt whizzed through the air.

14

"Let them rest until dawn, then we continue to—" Caden's words were abruptly cut off as his world erupted in pain.

Bast turned and shouted orders, but the words were an incoherent jumble. Caden looked down and saw a crossbow bolt protruding from his chest. His eyes traced the length of it, then further away to see where it had come from. Sitting astride Gedrith was Mina, crossbow in hand.

"Mina," he whispered, his voice barely audible over the shouts of the draman. Caden faltered and dropped to his knees. A wave of dizziness swept over him, and he collapsed onto his right side. His vision swam, and pain spread throughout his entire body.

"Caden."

He was vaguely aware of someone calling his name. Mina knelt at his side and touched his face. She had just shot him. Why was she acting as though she was now concerned?

"Caden," the voice wasn't hers. He blinked several times and realized it wasn't Mina beside him. It was Eira. Was he delirious?

"Hold him down," she said.

Bast's face appeared above him, and the draman motioned with his hand. Another draman joined him, and the two of them pinned Caden to the ground. Eira grabbed hold of the quarrel and jerked it free.

Caden roared in pain. He felt as though his flesh had been ripped apart, and wetness seeped through his shirt. He tried to lift his head, but another wave of dizziness forced him to lie still. Fire blazed in his blood, burning through every inch of his being.

"He's been poisoned," Eira said, looking at Bast. "This bolt looks like one of yours. Is it?"

The draman nodded. "Yes, it is ours. That blasted woman must have stolen it from one of my men."

"What girl?"

"It's a long story, one that can wait. We need to get him to Lireth."

"He'll be lucky if he survives the night, judging by his current state," Eira said. "Is there a physician among you?"

"There is, but he cannot do anything about this."

"Why not?"

"The poison is made from Lireth's blood. It is the source and the cure."

"You don't have any of it here?"

"No."

"I see. We should make him as comfortable as we can. If he pulls through until morning, that's something."

Caden's vision faded, and silence followed.

He floated in a sea of darkness, barely aware of his body. There was no pain, and he could breathe without effort, but his face and neck were numb. He tried to move his head, but his body didn't respond. Wherever he was, it was cold and empty. He tried to speak, but his mouth was locked shut.

A sound like creaking leather caught his attention. It got closer, and a feeling of warmth and comfort washed over him. He felt completely at peace. The warmth intensified, and Caden could feel his body loosen. He flexed his fingers, and they obeyed. Able to move now, he turned his head to look at his surroundings and saw Lireth. The rustling sound he heard was her wings. She towered over him, impressive and powerful.

Where am I? he asked. The words echoed all around them.

You are safe, she answered. *What happened?*

I was struck by an arrow.

A mere flesh wound would not send you here.

I think it had a poisoned tip. Mina—

Lireth rumbled angrily at her name. *She tried to kill you? I will burn this world to ash!*

Caden shrank back, fearful of her wrath. The soothing feeling returned, and he looked up at her. She had never been kind, at least not since she first called him to her cave in the mountains.

You are on the doorstep of death, she said.

Come to me, and I will heal you.

I don't know where you are.

When you reach The Long Sands, you will find guides. They are also allies. They will lead you to the Enclave. I will give you the strength to make the journey, but it will not be much. The distance between us is still too great. When you are closer, you will feel it.

Thank you, master.

My strength will only do so much. Your will to live must be great. Survive to avenge yourself.

Caden gasped and opened his eyes. He was lying in a tent. His head lolled weakly to the side, and he saw Rem was curled up nearby. The animal stared at him, deep intelligence behind its eyes. Hanging in the corner of the tent above the fox was a lantern. The flame burned steadily, providing plenty of light. Rem rose and stretched, then left the tent.

Caden could feel the dull pounding of a headache like a drum being played. He groaned, but the sound was weak and miserable. Why couldn't he move? Was it the effects of the poison?

Rem returned with Eira and Bast in tow. The draman stared down at him, his reptilian features creased into a smile, though it looked disturbing.

"You are strong, my lord. I am glad to see you are awake."

Caden licked his lips, but his mouth was dry and

it felt like he was rubbing sand together.

"Swallow," Eira said, kneeling beside him with a waterskin. She poured a small amount of water into his mouth. It was cool and refreshing, and it washed the dryness from his throat.

"How do you feel?" she asked.

"Like… death," Caden managed to whisper.

"The poison has spread through your body," Bast said. "It is potent."

"The d—desert." Even breathing was a chore, and it took all of Caden's effort to speak the words.

"We will continue our march at dawn, my lord. Finding Lireth is the only way to cure you."

"No. March… now. Time… is… short."

Eira looked up at Bast, but the draman ignored her.

"My lord, you need rest. You cannot even sit up, let alone walk."

"Lireth… sustains me. March… now."

The draman hesitated but bowed his head. "As you command." He left the tent and began shouting orders.

Eira poured more water into Caden's mouth. He swallowed it and stared at her, wondering why she hadn't returned to wherever it was she called home. She didn't owe him her loyalty. If anything, he owed her for helping him find the dragons.

"Rem says something odd was happening to you

while you were unconscious."

Caden nodded his head slightly, too exhausted to speak any more.

"Get some rest. You will need it. It will be a miracle if you are still alive in the morning. Rem will alert me if you need anything."

Eira stood and watched him for a moment, then backed out of the tent, leaving him with his thoughts and his pain. And Rem. The odd fox gazed at him knowingly.

15

Mina lay on her cot, staring up at the cave ceiling. The image of Caden being struck by the quarrel was burned into her mind. It haunted her the entire way back to the Enclave, and it haunted her even now, keeping her from sleeping.

She had killed him.

Tears stung her eyes. She knew it was the right thing to do, but she hated herself for doing it. And she hated herself for being upset about doing what was just. It was her fault he'd found Lireth in the first place. She'd used her newfound position with Lord Klodian to send him away. Now he was dead, and at her own hands.

Mina wiped the tears that trickled down her cheeks and sat up. It hurt, but her sadness wasn't going to bring him back. She needed to take her mind off things and allow her emotions to settle. Rising from the cot, she left her chamber and wandered along the tunnels. She tried to clear her mind, but it was impossible to erase Caden's stunned look from her memory.

"What doin'?"

Her heart leaped in her chest, and she whirled around to see Areg. He was barefoot and looked as though he hadn't been awake long.

"Did I wake you?" she asked.

Areg rubbed the sleep from his eyes and yawned. "No. What doin'?" he repeated.

"Nothing. Just …" Just what? She didn't know what to say, and an overwhelming wave of emotions crashed over her. She sank to the floor and began sobbing.

Areg drew near and embraced her, his small arms strong and comforting. He said nothing as she cried, and eventually, the tears stopped. Mina pulled away from the elf and wiped her eyes.

"Thank you," she said lamely, avoiding his gaze.

"What wrong?"

"My friend is … gone."

"Caden?"

Mina nodded, sniffling.

"It not good reply. But time heal."

He was right. It wasn't a good response, but she knew he was trying to help. And his words were true. Time healed wounds, though she knew this one would affect her for a long while. It all felt like a dream.

"Need rest. Battle coming."

"I can rest later. The draman are still at least a day's march from The Long Sands. Two days from here."

"They in desert now."

Mina looked at him. "That's impossible. They

stopped and set up—" Gedrith had been wrong. Removing their leader hadn't broken their ranks. "Does the Enclave know?"

Areg nodded. "Have time. You rest."

She was exhausted, but she doubted she'd be able to sleep. Despite that, she rose to her feet and walked with the elf to her chamber. Areg continued on his way, and Mina climbed onto her cot and tried to find solace in the darkness under her blanket.

Mina.

Someone was chasing her. It was a shadowy figure, the darkness of it constantly shifting about like dye poured into water.

Mina.

How did it know her name? She ran as fast as she could, but it was as though she moved through molasses. The darkness was closing in on her, wispy tendrils outstretched, reaching for her.

Mina.

She startled awake and kicked off the blanket. Sweat covered every inch of her body, and she realized there was nothing truly trying to get her. Gedrith was at the edge of her mind.

Are you all right? he asked. *The bond was filled with fear.*

I'm fine. It was a nightmare. I'm sorry.

Do not apologize. You cannot control your dreams. Prepare yourself and meet me above ground.

Mina dragged herself out of bed and donned her boots, followed by her armor. She buckled her sword around her waist and stepped out into the hall, pausing as her stomach rumbled. Breakfast could wait.

The tunnels were oddly silent as she made her way to the entrance of the underground fortress. When she climbed the steep slope and reached the top, she understood why. The dragons were all aboveground. Some were standing in the sand while others wheeled overhead.

What is it? Mina asked. She looked west, squinting.

The draman have arrived, Gedrith replied.

They traveled faster than I expected.

I'm sure Lireth had something to do with that.

She must have instructed them how to get here, too.

No, she does not know the way.

Then how did they know where to find us?

Come and see.

Mina climbed onto Gedrith's back and he took to the air. He didn't have to ascend far for her to see it. Numerous lines bulged in the sand, swaying back and forth.

Sand wyrms? But why—

They have aligned against a common enemy, Gedrith answered.

Mina stared in disbelief. At least a dozen of the creatures stirred up the sand, and behind them, the army of draman steadily marched closer. The dragons could easily defend against the smaller reptilians, but the sand wyrms posed a much bigger problem. This would not be an easy battle. She regretted not getting something to eat, but that was the least of her problems.

What's the plan?

We must keep them from reaching the tunnels. If they free Lireth, they will be emboldened.

You sound worried about that last part.

The scent of lavender reached her nostrils. Gedrith was afraid.

You don't think we can stop them? she asked.

I fear what we will lose with victory.

She didn't understand what he meant, and before she could ask, he said, *You will be on the ground. Focus your efforts on the draman. We will handle the sand wyrms.*

I would rather help you. I've killed a sand wyrm, and I can do it again.

The lavender smell turned to lemon and clove.

I do not doubt your abilities, Gedrith said. *But you must set your pride aside. In the time it takes you to kill one wyrm, we will have killed five. It is easier for me to fight with tooth, claw, and flame if I do not have to worry about you riding on my back.*

I understand, but what can I do against an army

of draman?

Whatever you must to keep them from getting inside the tunnels. Areg will help you, and once the wyrms are dealt with, we will turn our attention to them.

The sand wyrms were only a few hundred feet away, and a few of the dragons were making dives, raking their claws through the sand.

It is time, Gedrith said. He landed on the ground, and Mina quickly leaped from his back. *Stay alive.*

I'll do my best, Mina replied.

That's all I require from you.

He returned to the sky, and Mina felt some relief as Areg joined her. He wore a polished chainmail shirt, and the sunlight glinted off the rings, making it seem as though he was glowing. A sleek silver helm adorned his head, and the design etched into the metal was as beautiful as any piece of art. Wings stretched back on the sides, and the nose guard resembled an eagle's beak. He held on to the haft of a long spear, and a sword was sheathed at his waist.

"Don't you look regal," she said, grinning at him.

"Ready to die," he replied. "Impress ancestors."

Mina drew her sword and turned her attention to the advancing army. The dragons continued to harass the wyrms, but it didn't seem to slow their progress.

They're getting close to the tunnels, Mina warned Gedrith.

Just a little further, he said.

She tightened her grip on the hilt of her blade. How much further did they need to get? A tremor shook the ground, followed by another, and another.

"Stone wall," Areg said cheerily.

"What?"

The elf pointed to the ground. "Stone under sand. Big stone."

Mina laughed. The dragons had placed a wall of stone under the sand. It was a brilliant defense. One of the wyrms broke the surface of the ground, its fleshy body undulating as it rose up, up, up into the air.

The dragons attacked without mercy, breathing fire and slashing with their claws. The beast shrieked in anger and pain, its open maw snapping this way and that, trying to retaliate, but the dragons were too quick, easily maneuvering out of the way. Mina watched the display with admiration until Areg pointed with his sword.

The underground stone wall had stopped the advance of the wyrms, but the draman continued ahead, coming directly toward them. Mina's heart pounded in her chest, but oddly she didn't feel scared. She felt determined. She glanced over at Areg.

"Ready to make your ancestors proud?"

"With honor."

The draman were so close now that Mina could see the details of their reptilian faces. Their eyes blazed with battle lust, and they roared in challenge. Areg drew the spear back and threw it. It sailed through the air, striking one of the draman and sending him into a backflip. Adrenaline coursed through Mina, making her vision blur momentarily. It filled her with an odd mix of excitement and fear, and she let out her own battle cry.

An intense wave of heat washed over her as a dragon flew overhead, bathing the draman in a torrent of flames. Many of them fell, burned beyond recognition. Those that weren't continued ahead, clashing blades with her and Areg.

The elf moved with fluid grace, his sword weaving a deadly dance, cutting down draman after draman. Mina fought with all her might, the clashing of steel a constant noise, like the cadence of a war drum. She dodged attacks, parried with her sword, and landed blows of her own.

The battle raged on, but she and Areg were outnumbered. Mina wanted to risk a glance to see how the dragons fared against the wyrms, but she dared not lose her focus.

"Me! To me!" Areg shouted.

Mina back peddled in the direction of his voice until she bumped into him. They stood back-to-back, barely fending off the draman that surrounded them. From her periphery, she saw several of the creatures rush down into the tunnel. There was nothing they could do to stop them.

They're in the tunnel! she screamed at Gedrith.

He didn't respond, but she could feel his rage through the bond. The flapping of wings nearby made her flick her gaze up long enough to see a few dragons swooping in. Her relief faded when she realized they weren't allies.

Ignoring her and Areg, they landed in the sand and scrambled ahead, entering the tunnel. The draman would have trouble breaking the walls that contained Lireth, but not the dragons. Hope was fading, and with it, Mina's strength. Her movements became sluggish, and a draman got his blade past her parry, slicing the flesh on her left forearm. Burning pain spread up the length of her arm.

This was it. This was the end for her. For all of them. She thrust her sword into the neck of the draman who cut her, then screamed. All her fear, pain, and loss were behind her cry, but there was more. Something deeper, hotter. It yearned for freedom, and she allowed it to come forth.

Gedrith's fire poured from her mouth, engulfing the draman nearest to her. The flames continued unabated, and she turned her head left and right, burning everything in her path. Shrieks of pain and surprise filled the air, and the inferno drove the draman back.

The fire faded, and Mina dropped to her knees, the last of her strength expended. Her fingers were too weak to hold on to her sword, and it fell to the sand beside her. She had done all she could, and it still wasn't enough. Mina searched the sky for Gedrith. A few of the wyrms had fallen, but there were more alive than dead. There were so few dragons the sky looked empty to her.

The ground trembled, grains of sand vibrating against one another. Mina glanced around, confused, and met Areg's gaze. He looked toward the tunnel. She guessed more sand wyrms were coming. The vibration increased, growing stronger. Mina gathered what little vigor she could muster and grabbed her sword, slowly rising to her feet.

The earth above the cave system erupted, sand and glass flying in every direction. Lireth's enormous bulk flew up into the sky, her black scales dark as night. The dragon opened her mouth and issued an ear-piercing roar.

16

Caden lay on the slope of a dune and watched as the sand wyrms battled the dragons. As much as he would have preferred to be on the front lines with the draman, the poison running through his blood had wreaked havoc on him. When the sun rose, Eira and Bast were surprised to see he was still alive. If he were honest with himself, he was surprised as well. Despite Lireth's borrowed strength, it was all he could do to remain conscious.

"I've never seen anything like this," Eira said from beside him. "I didn't even know there was such a thing as a sand wyrm."

He didn't waste any words with her. His spirit was quickly fading. Although he'd made it through the night, he knew his time was running out.

Thank you for trusting me to lead your army, he told Lireth. *It has been an honor. They will free you soon, and you will get your vengeance upon the Enclave, but I fear I will not see it.*

You will not die. I will heal you.

Caden snorted a single laugh at the absurdity of her words. Surely, she could feel his connection to the bond slipping away. Or perhaps she was in denial, refusing to believe her servant was on the edge of dying. Either way, at least he'd had one final laugh before death took him. It felt good and temporarily drove the pain away, however brief.

"What is it?" Eira asked. "The dragon—Lireth?"

Caden nodded and felt his eyes lowering of their own will. He would have fought against it, but he didn't see the point. Rest was coming, and he welcomed it gladly. A flood of strength filled him, and he forced his eyes open. The battle was raging in every direction, and then Lireth burst out from the ground. His breath caught in his throat. She was majestic and beautiful.

I'm coming to you.

He wanted her to, but he knew it was a futile effort. Not even a dragon could defeat death. The dragons fighting the sand wyrms immediately broke away and flew straight for her.

A thunderous boom echoed off the dunes.

"The caves," Eira said. "They're collapsing."

Caden wondered if Mina was down there. He hoped so. She would die as he would, alone and forgotten. No family to mourn him, no friends to help him. Eira was a stranger, and Lireth … well, she was his master. There was no friendship between them. It was a bond of servitude. He saw that now, clearer than ever. Perhaps, in the end, Mina had been right.

He stared at the chaos unfolding and realized the truth. Lireth *was* evil. She had bound him to her without his knowledge or approval. Death, it seemed, brought clarity to many things. He deserved his fate, and he found it fitting the source of his death was poison made from the blood of the very creature who had saved him. Her call had been both a blessing and a curse.

And ultimately, he had failed. Not only Mina, but himself.

The thought of ceasing to exist, never to feel the touch of another, never again to be part of something more, never to atone for his wrongdoing filled him with grief and agony far more painful than the effects of the poison.

Lireth's strength began to fade again, and Caden felt something in the bond he never expected: anguish. And something else: guilt. Lireth felt guilty? That was the most surprising revelation of all.

He closed his eyes, and darkness enveloped him.

17

Gedrith and the other dragons who remained descended upon Lireth. The battle even consumed the attention of the draman. Mina kept her guard up, but the creatures were no longer concerned with her or Areg.

"What that?" the elf asked.

Mina turned to look in the direction Areg was pointing. Two figures were visible, away from the battlefield. The sunlight glared off the sand, and she squinted against the blinding light. Was that …

No. It couldn't be. He was dead. She's seen him fall with her own eyes. But she needed to be sure. She sprinted across the sand, and Areg followed after her. The draman ignored their departure, their focus still on their master.

As she drew closer, there was no mistaking it.

"Caden!"

Mina realized something was wrong. His flesh was pale, and he didn't seem to be conscious. A woman and a fox were with him, but she didn't recognize the person.

"Who are you?" the woman asked, stepping into her path.

"I'm a friend. Or, I was. Is he—"

"You're the one who struck him with the arrow,

aren't you?"

Mina's cheeks burned with guilt. "Yes, but you don't understand. He's—"

"I don't need to understand. You should leave. He's in enough agony from the poison. Let him die in peace."

"I need to speak to him," Mina protested. "Please."

The woman rested her hand on the hilt of her sword. "No. Now leave, before I make you."

Mina looked at Areg, and the elf nodded knowingly.

"I don't know your connection to Caden, but I know him better than you. He would want to speak with me."

The woman drew her sword, and the fox at her feet bared its teeth and hissed threateningly.

"I don't want to fight," Mina said.

"That makes one of us."

The woman lunged forward, the tip of her blade aimed at Mina's neck. Mina parried the strike, the sound of metal ringing through the air. The woman came at her with fury, and they clashed blades. The fox darted around Mina's feet, trying to trip her up, but Areg snatched it by the scruff of its neck and held on to it.

"Do not hurt Rem," the woman growled.

Mina could tell the woman was skilled, but she

was determined to get to Caden. She drew on Gedrith's strength, but she didn't pull much as she didn't want to disrupt his fight with Lireth. She siphoned just enough to invigorate her aching muscles and gain the advantage over the woman. Mina swung with all her might and shattered the woman's sword, just as she'd done to Caden in the forest.

The broken pieces of the blade fell onto the sand, and the woman hesitated. Mina sensed the woman had more fight in her, but she looked at her fox companion and backed down.

"I won't hurt him," Mina said. She stepped past her and knelt beside Caden. Areg had her back, so she wasn't concerned about the woman striking her when she wasn't looking.

"I'm sorry," she whispered. "I never meant for any of this to happen."

Tears slid down her cheeks, but she didn't bother to wipe them away. Caden didn't stir. She'd found him only to lose him again.

End him, Gedrith said to her. *It will weaken Lireth temporarily so we can defeat her.*

Mina froze and swallowed the lump in her throat. *Don't ask me to do this.*

I already did. Hurry!

She tightened her grip on the hilt of her blade, but she couldn't do it. It wasn't in her. Not this time. Not again. She dropped her sword and looked back at Areg.

"Must do."

"I can't," she whispered.

Areg started forward, but a noise like thunder cracked the sky. They both looked toward the battle. Lireth had unleashed some kind of magic, and it rippled across the sky. The surrounding dragons went limp and fell, crashing to the ground below. Her heart dropped into her stomach as she watched Gedrith spiral helplessly.

You must stop her!

Lireth bolted across the sky, faster than anything she'd seen before. The dragon opened her mouth, and flames poured out. Mina grabbed onto Areg and pushed him behind her, then summoned Gedrith's fire and breathed her own flames. The two streams collided in a blinding, searing display of power. Mina felt the heat on her skin, hotter than anything she'd encountered before. Sand and dust billowed into the air, and she gritted her teeth and pushed against Lireth's flames with all her might.

It wasn't enough.

Lireth's fire consumed hers, and the force threw Mina back, knocking the breath out of her. She gasped for air as she struggled to roll over. Her vision blurred and her head rang from the impact. Grit filled her mouth, but she didn't care about that. The dragon landed, and with a flap of her wings, she sent Areg and the woman tumbling along the dunes.

Mina's mind told her to get up, but her body

wouldn't obey. She watched, powerless, as Lireth stood over Caden's prone form.

Gedrith!

His answer was a flood of pain through the bond. She pushed it back, blocking off their connection. For a long moment, Lireth did nothing. She merely stood there, looking down at Caden. Finally, she lifted her head and opened her jaws. An ethereal tendril slipped out, white as smoke, and it drifted on the wind before snaking down into Caden's nostrils.

"No!" Mina screamed.

She tried standing, but her legs wouldn't hold her weight and she fell back onto the sand. Pushing through the pain, she crawled instead, desperate to reach Caden.

The last of the ghostly tendril escaped Lireth's mouth and disappeared into him. Mina didn't know what it was, but it couldn't be good. Lireth's legs shook, and the dragon fell on her side, blocking Caden from her view. Mina continued scrambling on her hands and knees, forced to go around the massive beast.

She reached Caden's side and laid her head on his chest. His heartbeat was faint. She looked at Lireth, worried she was going to get up and attack at any moment. The dragon breathed raggedly, and her eyes slowly closed. A final breath escaped her nostrils, and she lay still.

18

When Caden opened his eyes, the first thing he saw was the white ceiling above him. The second thing he saw was Eira. She sat at his bedside, and Rem was curled up in her lap. Her eyes were closed, but Rem was watching him.

Surprisingly, he felt no pain. He tried to flex his fingers—and it worked. He didn't feel weak, either. Caden pushed himself up on his elbow and looked around. He was in an infirmary. It looked vaguely familiar, but he wasn't sure where he was.

"You're awake." Eira smiled at him. "The physicians weren't sure if you'd come to. I'm glad you proved them wrong."

"W—where am I?"

"Klodian Keep. I've never heard of the place, but I'm not from this area."

Caden laid back down and stared at the ceiling. Klodian Keep? Had he dreamed everything? No, of course not. Eira and Rem were here, which meant it had all really happened. But the last thing he remembered was hazy. He'd been poisoned and was...

"What happened?"

"What do you remember?"

"Not much. Bits and pieces of the march to The

Long Sands. The wyrms were fighting the Enclave, and the rest is …" Caden shrugged. "Lost to memory."

"Lucky you. The draman freed Lireth from her prison. She battled with the Enclave before striking them all with a spell, then she stood over you and—" Eira looked off to the side, her eyes widening as if reliving the event, "—breathed something into you."

Caden repeated her words in his mind, trying to understand what it meant. Was it the cure for the poison? He reached through the bond, but there was nothing on the other end, just a vast abyss of emptiness.

"Where is she?"

"Mina?"

"What? No. Lireth. Where is Lireth?"

"She's … dead. Whatever she did saved your life and took hers."

At first, he felt the sting of agony. It slowly morphed into relief as fragments of his memory returned. He'd realized she was wicked, but given what he'd just learned, he questioned that. Would someone evil sacrifice themselves to save another? His first instinct was to say no, but perhaps he was wrong. Perhaps there was good in everyone, even if it was buried deep inside.

"You mentioned Mina. She survived?"

"Yes. She brought you here to heal. She brought

us, too, but Rem didn't exactly like riding on the back of a dragon. He said it was too windy."

Caden smiled. Mina had tried to kill him, and yet she went out of her way to bring him home, his true home. Another mystery to ponder.

"How do you feel?"

"Good. Normal."

With Lireth's presence completely gone from his mind, he felt as though a great fog had lifted. His thoughts were clear, and his own. He looked down at his body. There were no cuts or bruises, and his skin was tan and healthy. It was as if he'd never been poisoned—in body or in mind.

Eira watched him with a curious expression. Rem stretched and yawned, then jumped off Eira's lap to investigate the room.

"You seem … different."

"What do you mean?"

"I don't know. You seem centered. More in control. Of yourself, I mean."

It was true. He felt a newfound sense of clarity. Lireth must have been more in control of him than he'd known. It was a frightening realization. He sat up and inhaled a deep breath. Everything felt … fresh. It was like Lireth had breathed new life into him. Perhaps that was exactly what she did.

Caden swung his legs over the side of the bed and stood. Things would be different this time. They had to be. He looked at Rem, who was now inspecting a vase of flowers on the windowsill, then at Eira who was still staring at him.

"Thank you for your help. What will you do now? Go back to wilderness?"

Eira shrugged. "I thought about sticking around with you. It's been quite an adventure so far, so why stop now?"

Caden chuckled. "I've got to make some things right, and I don't know how exciting that will be, but you're welcome to stay around as long as you'd like."

Rem yelped, and Caden looked at the fox. "The same goes for you."

A long road lay ahead, but with his new friends, it didn't seem so daunting.

19

Mina sat outside the mountain cave, watching the stars twinkle above. Areg sat next to her, a wistful expression on his face. They couldn't be more different, the two of them. The Enclave decided to leave The Long Sands behind and build a new home closer to civilization.

Lireth was dead, but that didn't mean more threats wouldn't arise. In time, they would reintroduce themselves to humans, and possibly even rebuild the riders. Gedrith told her the Enclave was happy with her actions, and she had done much to restore their faith in humanity. The draman had fled after Lireth fell, their ranks broken and scattered.

She had left Caden in Lord Klodian's care, though in truth, she knew he was in better hands with Eira. The woman had tried to protect him from her, after all. She'd failed, but it was the effort that mattered.

"There's something I've been meaning to ask you," Mina said, glancing over at Areg.

"What?"

"Where are the rest of your people? Before I met you, I didn't even know elves existed."

"Far. Past ocean."

"Do you think you'll ever see them again?"

Areg shrugged. "Know not. Banished."

"They banished you?"

He nodded.

"For what?"

"Bond to dragon. Against law."

Mina's face scrunched in surprise. "I thought elves also bonded to dragons before the world forgot the truth about them?"

"Only humans forget. Elves know still. Royalty only bond to dragon. Areg not royalty."

Many things made sense with that knowledge, and Mina nodded in understanding. "I'm sorry for asking. I'm sure it hurts to talk about it. I was a slave, but at least I wasn't banished from my own kind."

"Long time. No pain."

Mina didn't know if she believed that, but she wasn't going to press him about it.

"What do?" he asked.

Mina looked back up at the stars and admired their beauty for a moment, then turned her gaze back to Areg.

"A wise friend of mine once told me what I should do, and I'm going to follow his advice."

The elf looked at her questioningly.

"He told me, 'Do good.' So I plan to do good every day until I no longer walk this world."

Areg grinned. "Plan good."

"I thought so, too."

Mina sighed. For the first time in a long time, she was content. All was well, and she was going to 'do good.'

THE END

ABOUT THE AUTHOR

Richard Fierce is a fantasy and space opera author. He's been writing since childhood, but began publishing in 2007. Since then, he's written multiple novels and short stories.

In 2000, Richard won Poet of the Year for his poem *The Darkness*. He's also one of the creative brains behind the Allatoona Book Festival, a literary event in Acworth, Georgia.

A recovering retail worker, he now works in the tech industry when he's not busy writing.

He's married and has three step-daughters (pray for him!), three grandchildren (he's young!), three dogs (huskies!), and two ferrets. He basically has a zoo.

His love affair with fantasy was born in high school when a friend's mother gave him a copy of *Dragons of Spring Dawning* by Margaret Weis and Tracy Hickman.

www.ingramcontent.com/pod-product-compliance
Lightning Source LLC
Chambersburg PA
CBHW021330060726
47591CB00006B/1956